For Jo and Mark ~ S P

LITTLE TIGER PRESS
An imprint of Magi Publications
1 The Coda Centre, 189 Munster Road, London SW6 6AW
www.littletigerpress.com

First published in Great Britain 2009

Text copyright © Magi Publications 2009 • Illustrations copyright © Simon Prescott 2009
Simon Prescott has asserted his right to be identified as the illustrator of this work
under the Copyright, Designs and Patents Act, 1988

A CIP catalogue record for this book is available from the British Library

All rights reserved • ISBN 978-1-84506-973-5

Printed in China

1 3 5 7 9 10 8 6 4 2

On A Dark Dark Night

Simon Prescott

LITTLE TIGER PRESS
London

In a dark, dark wood . . .

there was a dark, dark path.

Along the dark, dark path . . .

there was a dark, dark town.

In the dark, dark town . . .

there was a dark, dark street.

Down the dark, dark street . . .

there was a dark, dark gate.

Through the dark, dark gate . . .

there was a dark, dark yard.

In the dark, dark yard . . .

there was a dark, dark house.

In the dark, dark house . . .

there were some dark, dark stairs.

Down the dark, dark stairs . . .

there was a dark, dark room.

In the dark, dark room . . .

there was a dark, dark door.

And . . .

through the dark, dark door

there was . . .

. . . dinner!